ADVENTURES IN FRONTIER AMERICA

Flatboats on the Ohio

Westward Bound

by Catherine E. Chambers
illustrated by John Lawn

Troll

Dan Sawyer felt so good, this warm May morning of 1836, that he started to sing. The song he sang was all about the Ohio River.

Dan, his brother Joe, and his sister Martha used to sing that same song, back in Massachusetts. Everyone in New England knew about "Ohio fever." All over the East, word had spread about the fine soil and streams of the Ohio River valley, beyond the mountains. For twenty years now, families had been "westering," leaving the farms and towns of the East and moving out to the frontier.

This March, Pa had sold the Sawyers' farm to a cousin. He and Ma and the children had loaded furniture and clothing into the big new wagon with its canvas hood. Then they added tools, seed, and cuttings from the orchard. Ma had packed her best dishes in sawdust in a barrel. Chests held bedding and other household things. Ma sat on her rocker in the wagon, with Martha and Joe beside her. Dan was thirteen and the oldest. He got to sit on the wagon seat with Pa.

Today Pa was letting Dan drive the two gray horses. For five weeks the Sawyers had creaked uphill and down, through Connecticut and New York. Then they went by ferry-raft across the Hudson River to New Jersey. Their travel took them through town and country, sleeping in roadside inns, the farmhouses of friendly settlers, or in the wagon. The younger children were sometimes frightened by the woods at night, but Dan loved them. He loved helping Pa and being outdoors.

Even in the raw mid-Pennsylvania country, they met other travelers every day. These were the years of the Great Migration that was opening up America's frontier. Some families traveled in open ox carts. Some were in one-seater buggies with baggage tied on top. Some were on horseback. Some were on foot, pushing their belongings in wheelbarrows. When they met, they shared news of where the best land was, and whether the road ahead was rough or smooth.

Now the Sawyer wagon was rolling down Third Brother Mountain. Pittsburgh and the Ohio River lay close ahead, and Dan had good reason to feel like singing.

At last, far below them, they saw the roofs of Pittsburgh shining against the sky. "See how the three rivers meet?" Pa said, pointing. "The near one from the north is the Allegheny. The river from the south is the Monongahela. And the big one ahead is the Ohio. In Pittsburgh, you'll have three kinds of water to wash your faces."

"Monongahela, Monongahela," Martha crooned, making a song of it. "That's a pretty name."

"It's an Indian name," Pa said. "But we don't have to expect trouble from Indian tribes. The Ohio River's pretty safe nowadays because there's lots of traffic on it. A few years back, river boats had to be built like forts."

Pittsburgh in 1836 was a bustling city of more than twenty thousand people. Along the river banks were many businesses—potteries, brickyards, and gristmills. "Tomorrow we'll look for boatyards and sawmills," Pa said to Dan. "We have to get ourselves a boat. But right now, let's find a place to stay."

The streets of Pittsburgh were crowded with wagons—lumber wagons, farm wagons, freight wagons with blue sideboards and red wheels. Pa went into an inn and came out again. "Full up," he said. The same thing happened at the next inn and the next. Some of the inns by the boat landings Ma wouldn't let him try. They were ramshackle and dirty, and rough-looking rivermen stood about. Finally, Pa came out of a pleasant-looking yellow building and told Ma to climb down. They and the younger children went inside while Dan took care of the horses in the yard of the inn.

All the Sawyers would sleep together in one room, as families usually did. Pa and Ma would have the bed with its blue-checked covers, while the children slept on a low trundle bed on the floor. But first they had their supper in

6

the inn's common-room. This was a cheerful place lit by candles in tin holders hanging from the ceiling. When Dan came in, he found his family at a long table talking with a young couple.

"These are the Beebes," Pa said. "They're going down-river too. They'd like to share a flatboat with us."

7

Dan knew it took three men to navigate a flatboat. The boats were as big as cabins. Flatboats were difficult to handle because they were at the mercy of the river's currents. Rich people hired boatmen who knew the river. Other folks tried to manage on their own. Boats could be wrecked on sandbars or on "snags." These were logs or even whole trees embedded in the river.

"I've done some boating on the Ohio," Luke Beebe told the Sawyers. "Today I bought a booklet that shows a map of the river from here to the Mississippi." He spread it on the table, and Dan and the others looked at it eagerly. On each left-hand page was a map of a section of the river, and on the right was a description of what to watch for.

"I can help you with the poling," Luke said to Dan and Mr. Sawyer. "You'll need a third man aboard. It would be hard for Clara and me to build a raft and go down-river on our own. Clara can help Mrs. Sawyer with house-keeping on the trip."

"We'll talk about it in the morning," Pa said. Dan knew that meant Pa and Ma were first going to talk it over that night. He could see, though, that Pa and Ma already liked the Beebes. So did he.

8

In the morning Pa and Luke and Dan walked down to the river. Pa had already decided they would buy a boat instead of making one. "I have money from selling the farm to Cousin Joseph. If we buy a boat, we can begin the trip in a week or so. If we stop to build one, it could take all summer."

"When you get to where you're going, you'll be able to live in your boat till you build yourselves a house," the boatwright told them. "Then you can sell the boat to someone else. Or you can take it apart and use the planks for building."

10

When Dan saw his first flatboat he understood why. It was really a whole house, built on a shallow rectangular boat called a *scow*. The walls of the house were lined up with the sides of the boat and were made of four-inch-thick planks. The roof, too, was four inches thick. It had a very shallow pitch and could serve as a deck, for a ladder inside the cabin led to a trap door.

In the *stern*, or rear, was a stable for the animals. On the other side of the wooden partition, or *bulkhead*, was a storeroom. In front, or *forward*, canvas partitions divided the space into staterooms, a galley kitchen, and a "setting room." There was even a stone fireplace for heat and cooking.

"I like this boat," Pa decided. "It's not too big and not too small. It will hold five Sawyers and two Beebes just fine."

"It'll cost you one hundred sixty dollars," the boatwright said. "Four dollars per foot, and this one's forty feet long. Some of the big boats go up to sixty feet."

"That would be big enough to hold Noah and all the animals," Pa said chuckling. "This one only has to be *Sawyer's Ark*." He paid the money, counting the amount out carefully.

There were many things to do before they could leave. First, all the baggage from the wagon was loaded aboard. Then Pa sold the wagon. There was food to buy, and wood for the stove. Ma bought some chickens. "They'll give us eggs for the children's breakfast," she said firmly when Pa laughed.

12

"We should buy a cow, too," Pa said. "We'd best do that at some farm down-river. The price won't be so high."

Within two weeks, the Beebes and Sawyers were ready to leave. Dan helped walk the horses up the gangplank. Joe and Martha followed, each carrying a chicken. The Beebes' two horses went on board, too. Then Luke Beebe went to the roof and took hold of the great paddle. The handle was as long as the boat itself.

"Cast off!" Luke said, and Pa did so. The flatboat moved off into the green-brown water. Everyone climbed up on the roof to watch as they moved downstream.

The Ohio River was the great "moving highway" to the West during the years of the Great Migration. Dan was surprised at how many different kinds of boats he saw. There were flatboats large and small. There were rafts made of logs, often with a log cabin in the middle. Some boats even had a covered wagon on them. And there were large cargo flatboats manned by rivermen.

"They're going down to New Orleans," Luke told Dan. "Then the cargo goes by ocean ship to Mexico or Europe. The cargo boat's sold for firewood. The crew works its way back up the Mississippi on a keelboat. It takes a lot of men to move a keelboat upstream."

A keelboat was a long, narrow craft that came to a point at one or both ends. Unlike a flatboat, it did not have a flat bottom. Keelboats had four or more oarsmen on each side, and they also had a mast and sail. The smallest were called keels and could carry twenty-five tons of freight. Barges were larger, and packet boats that carried passengers were largest of all. On the back, or *aft*, deck of a keelboat was a platform, or *pulpit*, on which the steersman stood. He held the handle of a wide-bladed oar that acted as a rudder.

Pa pointed out a long, long boat with a cabin like the *Ark*'s and two masts and a smokestack belching smoke. "That's a steamboat! There have been steamboats traveling to New Orleans since 1811!" Martha's and Joe's eyes grew large, but Ma shuddered. "You couldn't pay me to ride on those newfangled things! Suppose the boiler blew up?" She liked better to watch the little boats that moved along the river like water beetles. There were *sneakboxes*, little scows with just a steering oar. And there were odd-looking little rafts with a haystack on one end and a tent on the other.

After a few days, life on *Sawyer's Ark* fell into a pattern. In pleasant weather Dan let the horses out on the back deck to graze on a mound of hay. The chickens were supposed to eat there, too, but they liked it better on the roof. They would flutter up and poke into whatever games the children played. Sometimes they flew down to the front deck to sit with Ma and Clara Beebe as they washed clothes or peeled potatoes or sewed. Ma had a clothesline strung between two poles on the roof.

Once in a while, parakeets or wild turkeys would light on the *Ark* to eat the chickens' feed. One day a rooster flew over from another flatboat. He strutted, ruffling his lion's mane of rust-red feathers, and his tailfeathers gleamed in the sun.

There were people to visit with, too, along the river. Folks on the other boats waved and called greetings. Sometimes Dan saw a farmer plowing on the river bank or a woman looking at them from a cabin door. In the evening, Pa or Luke would steer for shore. Dan would tie the *Ark* to a willow tree. Sometimes the men went hunting. Sometimes they dropped their fishing lines over the side.

Martha liked to fish, too. She was very proud when she caught a perch for Ma's frying pan. Ma and Clara cooked supper in the cabin fireplace, but the travelers often ate outdoors. Some nights, folks from a riverside house might come down to visit. Later they would sit watching the stars reflected in the quiet water. They could hear the splash of oars as a freightboat passed, and the sad note of the horn.

Day followed day. *Sawyer's Ark* drifted with the tide along the Ohio's many twists and turns. Now, often, there were no settlements along the shore. When the woods were very dark and silent, several families would lash their boats together for the night. This was called "rafting up." After supper, there would be singing and dancing and story-telling. Sometimes rivermen from the freight barges would hear the music and come ashore, too. Dan loved to hear their talk. There were Frenchmen from the fur-trading posts up north, and even some Ring-Tailed Roarers. Those were swaggering Kentuckians who claimed to be part-horse, part-alligator. They loved to brag as much as they loved to fight. Ma usually dragged the children off to bed as soon as any Ring-Tailed Roarers came around.

18

Often Dan heard tales of how thirty or forty years ago,
"ghost boats" had been found abandoned at the riverside.
The families had gone ashore and were never seen again.
Perhaps Indians had attacked. Today danger from Indians
was past. But there was still danger from the river, the
Ring-Tailed Roarers said. Great "ghost" trees could rise up
suddenly in front of you, or giant hands reach out to grab
your boat. Dan did not believe it.

After two weeks, the *Ark* reached Cincinnati. This port was a big city of more than twenty-five thousand people. When Pa tied up, a lot of "river rats" came around at once. They were men who lived off the river, working here and there, buying and selling and trading and maybe stealing. A few of them offered to buy the *Ark*.

The grownups held a conference. "There's good land around here still," Pa said. "But I hear there's even prettier land down below the Louisville Falls. Warmer winters there, too."

Everyone decided that the *Ark* would go on its way. The Sawyers and Beebes only went ashore to buy provisions. Ma didn't like the city. There were too many people and too many mosquitoes for her taste.

After Cincinnati, the river twisted and turned some more. The days were hot in June. Everyone was growing lazy. "That's the rhythm of the river," Ma said, smiling. "It will be hard working sunup to sundown again once we're ashore." But in the meantime, life was pleasant.

Daylight was long now. The *Ark* floated for an hour or more after supper. One clear night Pa said, "We might as well keep drifting. The river's smooth as glass. We don't have to worry about reaching the Louisville Falls till day after tomorrow."

After another hour, Dan saw Pa yawn. "Let me steer, Pa!" he said. "You said yourself the river's smooth tonight."

"Just for a while," Pa said. "I'll be on deck."

Pretty soon Dan heard Pa snore. He didn't wake him. This was his chance to show what he could do. The moonlight wasn't bright enough to read the chart by, but Dan had studied it carefully earlier. There were no sandbars or rapids in the way.

It was so peaceful on the roof at night. Dan looked for the Big Dipper and for Orion. The stars twinkled back at him in a friendly way. The French travelers had told him how they plotted their way by the stars in the great Northwest. Maybe one day he, too, would be a riverman and work his way clear down to New Orleans. It sounded a lot more exciting than farming.

Suddenly, Dan heard a noise. *Cr-r-ack!* Something was breaking. Wood. It was the boat. The *Ark* lurched sharply, then settled back. Pa woke with a shout. *"What happened?"*

"I don't know!" Dan shouted back. The skin on his neck felt like it was crawling. The *Ark* wasn't drifting anymore. It bobbled up and down, jolted by the current.

Pa's face appeared through the trap door, gaunt in the moonlight. He was followed by Luke. "I'll get the lantern," Luke called, and disappeared. Pa grabbed the oar-pole out of Dan's hands and worked with it frantically, but the *Ark* would not budge. From the cabin Dan could hear the women's anxious voices. The children awoke and started to cry.

"Don't be afraid," Dan shouted hoarsely. He wished he could follow his own advice.

Luke came walking across the roof, the lantern swaying. It sent yellow fingers out into the dark—and showed gray fingers gripping the *Ark* tightly. The hair on the back of Dan's neck stood up.

"It's one of those ghost trees we heard about," cried Dan. Luke lifted the lantern high. A dead tree that was very real stuck up out of the water. The *Ark*'s prow was impaled on the branches.

"A snag," Pa said heavily. "I thought we'd been very lucky up till now. I can't understand why it wasn't shown on the chart."

Dan's voice cracked. "Pa, I'm sorry...I guess I wasn't watching."

"No use crying over spilt milk," Pa said. He and Luke jumped down to the front deck to see how bad the damage was.

"We're close to shore," Luke said at last. "We're not leaking water. The hole's above the water line. We'd better leave well enough alone till daylight."

24

"I'll sleep on the roof," Dan said quickly. "So we'll know if anything more goes wrong." But Pa and Luke took no chances. They stayed there, too.

When gray light began to show above the tree tops, they all climbed down. A big tree pointed upstream from beneath the water. It rose and fell slowly with the current, and the *Ark* rose and fell along with it. Luke started to laugh. "You know what you're stuck on, Mr. Sawyer? That's a 'sawyer' down there!" That meant a tree that went up and down like a saw in a sawmill because it was not embedded in the earth. "Planters" were trees or logs firmly rooted in the riverbed. "Sleepers" were those invisible beneath the water.

"Ahoy!" A voice trumpeted to them down the quiet river. A large flatboat was coming towards them through the dawn. A big man was steering, and a boy and girl Dan's age were running forward on the roof. The *Roberts' Folly* pulled up alongside the *Ark*, and Dan and young Jim Roberts tied the boats together. Jim's father, Mr. Roberts, came over to inspect the damage.

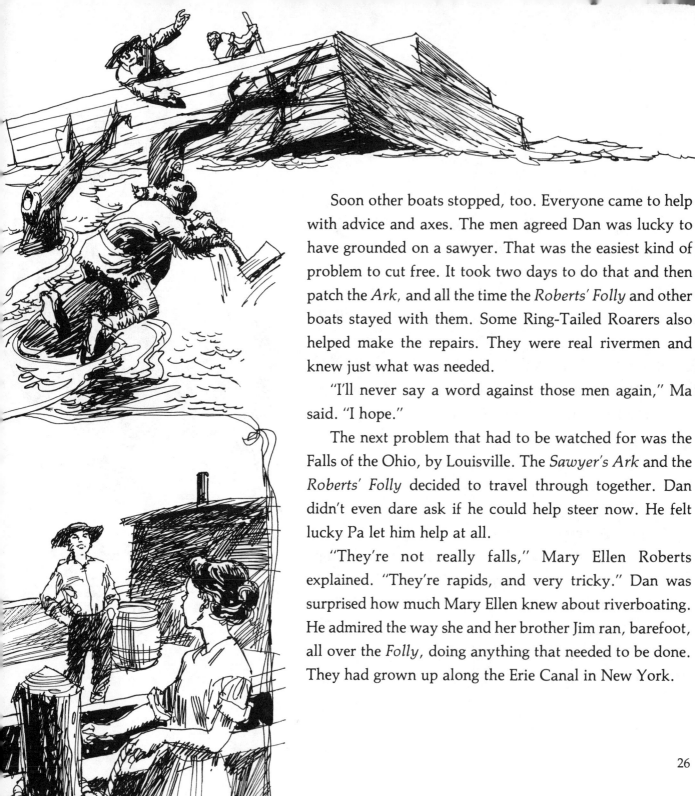

Soon other boats stopped, too. Everyone came to help with advice and axes. The men agreed Dan was lucky to have grounded on a sawyer. That was the easiest kind of problem to cut free. It took two days to do that and then patch the *Ark,* and all the time the *Roberts' Folly* and other boats stayed with them. Some Ring-Tailed Roarers also helped make the repairs. They were real rivermen and knew just what was needed.

"I'll never say a word against those men again," Ma said. "I hope."

The next problem that had to be watched for was the Falls of the Ohio, by Louisville. The *Sawyer's Ark* and the *Roberts' Folly* decided to travel through together. Dan didn't even dare ask if he could help steer now. He felt lucky Pa let him help at all.

"They're not really falls," Mary Ellen Roberts explained. "They're rapids, and very tricky." Dan was surprised how much Mary Ellen knew about riverboating. He admired the way she and her brother Jim ran, barefoot, all over the *Folly*, doing anything that needed to be done. They had grown up along the Erie Canal in New York.

That night everyone gathered in the Robertses' setting room to study charts of the river. Everyone learned what his or her job would be when they reached the rapids. Even little Martha and Joe had a job—they were told to keep an eye on the chickens in the stable. "That will keep them out of trouble, too," Ma said with relief.

It was hard to make the *Ark* go through the rapids at the proper angle and to avoid shallow spots where they could go aground. Dan worked until his arms ached. When at last the *Ark* and the *Folly* were tied for the night below the rapids, he felt as if he'd made up a little for the sawyer.

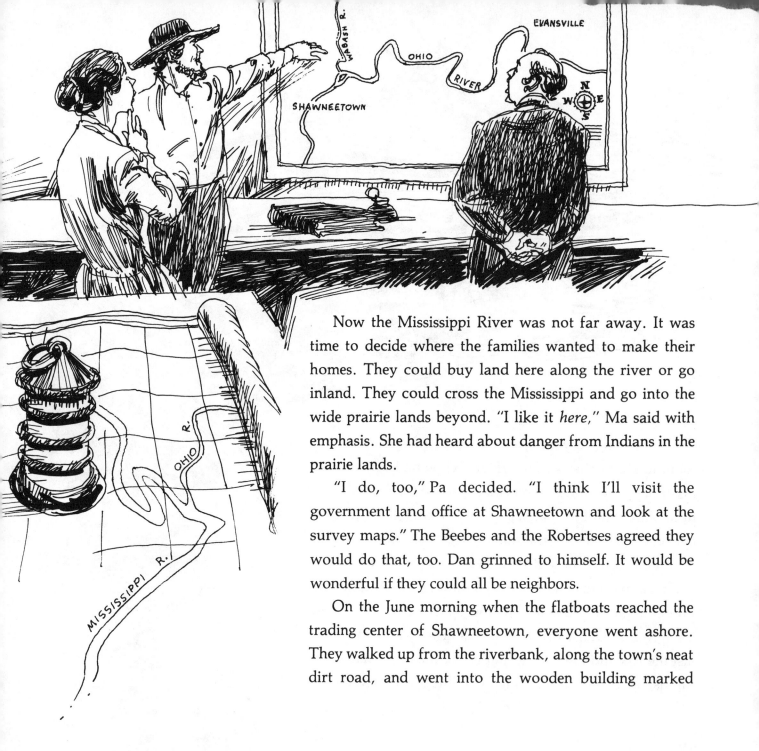

Now the Mississippi River was not far away. It was time to decide where the families wanted to make their homes. They could buy land here along the river or go inland. They could cross the Mississippi and go into the wide prairie lands beyond. "I like it *here*," Ma said with emphasis. She had heard about danger from Indians in the prairie lands.

"I do, too," Pa decided. "I think I'll visit the government land office at Shawneetown and look at the survey maps." The Beebes and the Robertses agreed they would do that, too. Dan grinned to himself. It would be wonderful if they could all be neighbors.

On the June morning when the flatboats reached the trading center of Shawneetown, everyone went ashore. They walked up from the riverbank, along the town's neat dirt road, and went into the wooden building marked

28

"Land Office." The big square room had large survey maps pinned to the wall. They showed, in square-mile sections, all the streams and rivers, high lands and low. They showed what was forest and what was meadow. The ledgers on the counter showed what land had already been sold.

"I want to be near the river," Mr. Roberts said, and Pa agreed. Then they could live on the boats until their houses were built. And they wouldn't need to build wagons right away. Pa picked out a section on the Wabash River near where it joined the Ohio. The Beebes and the Robertses picked out land nearby. The price of public land was two dollars an acre, and Pa's section came to one hundred sixty acres. Pa was able to pay cash, because he had money from the sale of the Massachusetts farm. Mr. Roberts paid cash, too. Luke took eighty dollars from his wallet. He watched the land agent mark "A.P."—advance paid—against his name. Then the men signed the ledger. The land agent gave Pa and Mr. Roberts deeds to their land. He gave Luke a certificate that he could exchange for a deed when all his payments were made.

That night the Beebes, the Robertses, and the Sawyers tied their boats to willow trees on their own land. Much work lay ahead. Meadowland had to be plowed and crops planted, for it was already June. Until that was done, and perhaps longer, they would live on their boats. Then the boats would be taken apart and the wood used to build houses. "We'll want smooth boards," Ma said firmly. "Like on the *Ark*. Not rough logs. You can keep them for the barn! And I surely would like a porch looking out on the river."

It would be a year before those houses would be finished—a year before Mrs. Roberts had a setting room like she had had back home, with the lace curtains and the small organ called a melodeon she had brought along. But on this June night, with Mary Ellen playing the melodeon in the *Folly's* setting room, and everybody singing as the sun went down, Dan thought life was fine just the way it was.

30

Index

activities on flatboat journey, 16–18, 21
Allegheny River, 5

barge, 15
belongings taken to frontier, 3
Big Dipper, 22
boats, different kinds on river, 14–15
boatwright, 10, 11
buying land:
  government land office, 28–29
  survey maps, 29
  deed, 29

Cincinnati, Ohio, 21

danger:
  from dead trees, 8, 23–25
  from Indians, 5, 19, 28

Erie Canal, New York, 26

ferry-raft, 4
flatboat, 7, 14
  activities on board, 16–18, 21, 30
  cost of, 11
  description of (bulkhead, forward, stern), 11
  great paddle, 13
  loading of, 12–13
  navigation of, 8, 22

stuck on dead tree, 23–25
use as home, 10, 29, 30
French fur traders, 18, 22

"ghost boats" and "ghost trees," 19, 24
government land office, 28–29
Great Migration, 4, 14

houses, building of, 10, 30
Hudson River, 4

Indians, dangers from, 5, 19, 28
inn, staying at, 4, 6–7

keel, 15
keelboat, 14
  description of (aft, pulpit), 15

Louisville Falls, 21, 22, 26
  navigating, 27

melodeon, 30
Mississippi River, 8, 14, 28
Monongahela River, 5

New Orleans, Louisiana, 14, 15, 22

"Ohio fever," 3
Ohio River, 3, 5, 8, 14, 18, 29
Orion, 22

packet boat, 15
Pittsburgh, Pennsylvania:
  businesses of, 6
  three rivers of, 5
"planter" (dead tree), 25
prairie lands (west of Mississippi), 28

"rafting up," 18
Ring-Tailed Roarers (Kentuckians), 18–19, 26
"river rats," 21
route west, 4–5

"sawyer," (dead tree), 25, 26
scow, 11
Shawneetown, Illinois, 28
"sleeper" (dead tree), 25
"snag," 8, 24
sneakbox, 15
stars, navigation by, 22
steamboat, 15
survey maps, 29

Third Brother Mountain, 5
trees, as danger to boats, 8, 23–25

vehicles for land travel, 4

Wabash River, 29
"westering," 3

This edition published 1998 by Troll Communications L.L.C.

Printed in the United States of America.

10   9   8   7   6   5   4   3   2

Cover art by Robert F. Goetzl.

Library of Congress Cataloging-in-Publication Data

Chambers, Catherine E.
    Flatboats on the Ohio.

    (Adventures in frontier America)
    Summary: In 1836, the Sawyers leave Massachusetts
to travel to the Ohio River valley for the beginning of a
new life.
    [1. Frontier and pioneer life—Ohio—Fiction.   2. Flat-
boats—Fiction.   3. Ohio River valley—History—Fiction]
I. Lawn, John, ill.   II. Title.   III. Series: Chambers,
Catherine E. Adventures in frontier America.
PZ7.C3558Fl   1984   [Fic]   83-18278
ISBN 0-8167-0049-4 (lib. bdg.)
ISBN 0-8167-4890-X (pbk.)